Chase and Mark would always
meet at the park after school
as they were best friends.

They never did anything without each
other! They were like two peas in a pod.

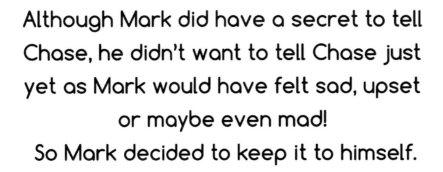

Although Mark did have a secret to tell
Chase, he didn't want to tell Chase just
yet as Mark would have felt sad, upset
or maybe even mad!
So Mark decided to keep it to himself.

Summer was always an enjoyable season for the boys! They loved swimming, playing tennis, drinking soda, and eating their favorite chocolate ice cream cones!

They would go to each other's houses, and play video games. Life was the best when Mark had Chase, and Chase had Mark.

Suddenly, Mark got an important
phone call from his mother.
"Mom?" Mark said on the phone,
"I need you home, like right now!"
Mark's mom said on the phone,
"Okay mom." Mark replied.

"Mark? Everything ok!?" Chase asked.

"Yeah! We're all fine." Mark said.
Chase hesitated in asking Mark to keep playing
video games with him, but he could tell that Mark
didn't look happy.
"I have to go home, sorry bud!"
Mark said with a tear dropping down his eye,
he immediately wiped it...

"Aw, we were just about to finish the round!"
Chase whined. "I know, but we have all summer!"
Mark cheered him up. "You're right." said Chase,
and off Mark went.

As he walked home, he kept thinking about telling Chase about his secret and about his reactions. Would he be mad, sad, or glad? He didn't know...

Soon Mark arrived home.
"Oh you're finally here! Nice timing Mark!
I need you to pack some of your clothes!"
said Mark's mom.

"Huh? Mark said,
"Aren't we moving next week?"
Mark said, confused.
"No, we are moving tomorrow!"
Mark's mom said happily.

Mark was in deep trouble, he didn't know how to tell
Chase his secret - that he was moving to a new town!
He had to tell Chase by today or tomorrow morning.

Maybe he could just forget about it and still go to
Chase's house and not tell Chase anything.
There was no way that Mark could keep
that secret from Chase!
There was absolutely no way!

So Mark gave Chase a call,
"Hey bud!" Chase answered.
"Hi" Mark replied.
"I have a secret Chase!"

"Oh what is it?" Chase asked.
"Well, tomorrow I am moving to a new town!
But we can still play at each other's houses, my adress is-"
Chase hung up the call, when Mark was
about to say his address.

"Chase?!" Mark cried. He would never know
Mark's address now... Slowly the sun went down,
and the moon came up and it was bedtime but
Mark couldn't sleep. He was worried.

He stayed in his room watching TV hoping Chase would call. He had tried calling Chase, but there was no answer. It was 12 am in the morning, what would Mark do tomorrow? It was moving time at 9am.

Then the sun came up and the moon went down! It was 7 am and Mark's family was chit-chatting about the new house!

Mark did smile a little bit. Their new house had a pool in the backyard and Mark was going to have a bigger room!

But he wasn't glad about his new school. He didn't want to be the new kid. He wanted his old friends back, not new friends.

But he knew the line 'the more the merrier', which meant, the more people the better time you will have.

Mark always said that to himself when he felt lost.
Mark texted Chase,
"Leaving now, goodbye!
"Good-Bye house!" "Good-bye town!"

Mark yelled and off they went.
They were driving in a moving van,
Mark was looking out the window.

Then he saw Chase!
Chase had a sign that said,
"WE WILL MISS YOU! GOODBYE!!"

Mark's parents saw the sign.
They opened the window and said,
"Thank you!"

When they got to the house,
there was a lot of setting up to do.
But they got it done in no time!

TWO MONTHS LATER...
After a while, Mark had his whole room set up!
His mom and dad's room, and the guest bedrooms!
Mark didn't regret moving at all!

Mark would call Chase every day, but Mark couldn't go to his house every day. He had to get used to some things in life, different neighborhoods, and different rules!

Then after a week,
Chase didn't call Mark on Saturday.
Sadly, he was wondering 'why not?',
but then there was a knock on his door.

"Go answer it Mark!" His dad yelled at him, so he did.
"CHASE? BUDDY!!!" Mark yelled so hard, and gave him a
big hug! Mark's parents planned a great surprise for
him as they knew that they were such good friends.
"I have a surprise for you."
Chase handed Mark a gift bag.

"No way! A video game, the one I always wanted!"
Mark yelled, once again.
"Let's go play it! Thank you so much Chase!"
Mark thanked him. He was happier than a baby with candy. Mark may have moved, but that doesn't stop him from having a best friend that lives in a totally different neighborhood!

Dedications & Acknowledgements

I would like to dedicate this book to my mom and my dad. Thank you for always being there for me and for your unconditional love and support along the way. You've taught me to strive for excellence and never accept anything less than extraordinary. I will continue to pursue my passion and chase my dreams. Love you both!

I would also like to thank all my teachers that I've had in each of the schools that I've attended so far. Thank you for all your encouragement and inspiration that led me to take this step towards publishing my first book. I shall remain forever grateful to each one of you!

Special thanks to my illustrator Sofie Engstrom Von Alten as well! Thank you for adding wonderful colors to my story and bringing it to life. I appreciate all the hard work you put in and your attention to detail. It has been a pleasure to work with you!

About the Author

Myra Manji is a rising 6th grader at William Annin Middle School in Basking Ridge, NJ. She lives there with her dad, mom, brother Naail and their 2 year old King Charles Cavalier Spaniel, Zoey. She loves, baking, painting, traveling with her family and spending time with her friends.

Made in the USA
Las Vegas, NV
06 March 2024

86816042R00024

The End.